magic carpet ride ☆☆ ☆☆
☆☆
REMAIN SEATED WHILE
CARPET IS IN FLIGHT

25m

City Swim Centre
Family Splash Session
VALID ON: FRIDAY

ORDER ID:

TOP:CARD
ode:4
ate: Discount:
                Tran:194332   1 adult
             Time:11:11   1 child
                        Serial:500836
                        Cashier:5137

Tickets are non refundable, non transferable and not for resale. Guests who impede the safety or enjoyment of other visitors, and do not follow instructions provided by members of staff, may be

PUBLIC LIBRARY
Membership Card

Barcode: 6FK23X

Signature: Tilly   Membership no:

First published in 2014 by Child's Play (International) Ltd
Ashworth Road, Bridgemead, Swindon SN5 7YD UK

Published in USA by Child's Play Inc.
250 Minot Avenue, Auburn, Maine 04210

Distributed in Australia by Child's Play Australia Pty Ltd
Unit 10/20 Narabang Way, Belrose, NSW 2085

Text and illustrations copyright © 2014 Gillian Hibbs
The moral right of the author and illustrator has been asserted

ISBN 978-1-84643-601-7

CLP121113CPL12136017

Printed and bound in Shenzhen, China

1 3 5 7 9 10 8 6 4 2

A catalogue record of this book is available from the British Library

www.childs-play.com

Tilly's Staycation

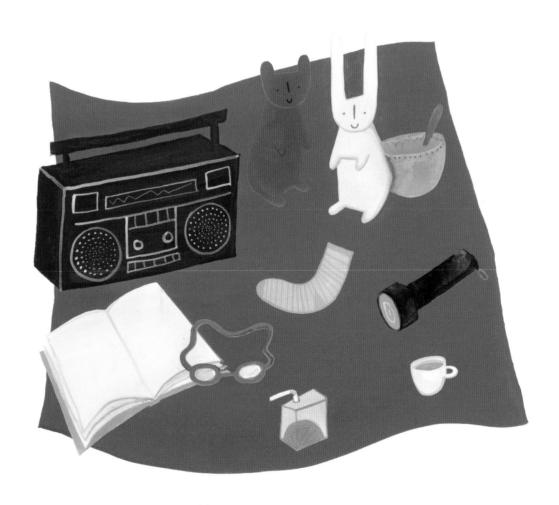

Gillian Hibbs

"Why can't **we** go on vacation?" asked Tilly.

"Tariq is going to India,

Paris is going to Paris,

and Tim is going camping."

Rory is going to the ocean,

Chanel is going to Florida,

"We'll have just as much
fun as everyone else, you'll see,"
Mom answered. "Maybe more!"

That night, Tilly went to have dinner with Paris. Her mom was packing a huge suitcase full of all the things they needed for their vacation.

Back home, Tilly had
a sneaky look to see if Mom
was packing the old suitcase
they sometimes took to visit Granny.
It was sitting on top of the chest of
drawers gathering dust, just like it always did.

The next day,
Tilly walked home from
school with Tariq and his dad.
"Who's he talking to?" whispered Tilly.
"The travel agent," replied Tariq.
"He's sorting out the flights for tomorrow."

At home, the phone rang.

"Hello Granny,"
Tilly sighed disappointedly.
"I thought you might have been
the travel agent."

Tilly was really down in the dumps.
"It's my vacation and I'm not
doing anything at all!" she sniffed.
But she couldn't help hoping that

**something exciting might
be about to happen,**

and went to sleep with
a little tingle in her toes.

The next morning, Tilly was
allowed to have breakfast in Mom's bed,
just like she did on her birthday!

"Get your best adventuring clothes on,
My Little Explorer," Mom smiled.
"We've got a bus to catch!"

When they got off the bus, Tilly was puzzled.
"Why have you brought me to the library?" she asked.

BUS STOP

SPACE
KINGS AND QUEENS
UNICORNS
PENGUINS

It was a hot day outside, but the library was cool, breezy and peaceful.

Mom told Tilly stories of faraway places and marvellous people. They were worlds away...

...fighting dragons,
sailing pirate ships,
meeting princesses...

TO THE PARK

...and hiding from **ferocious beasts.**

Then it was time to stop for a well-earned lunch in a Top Secret Hideaway...

TO THE SWIMMING POOL

...before discovering
hidden treasure and rare sea creatures.

TO THE MARKET

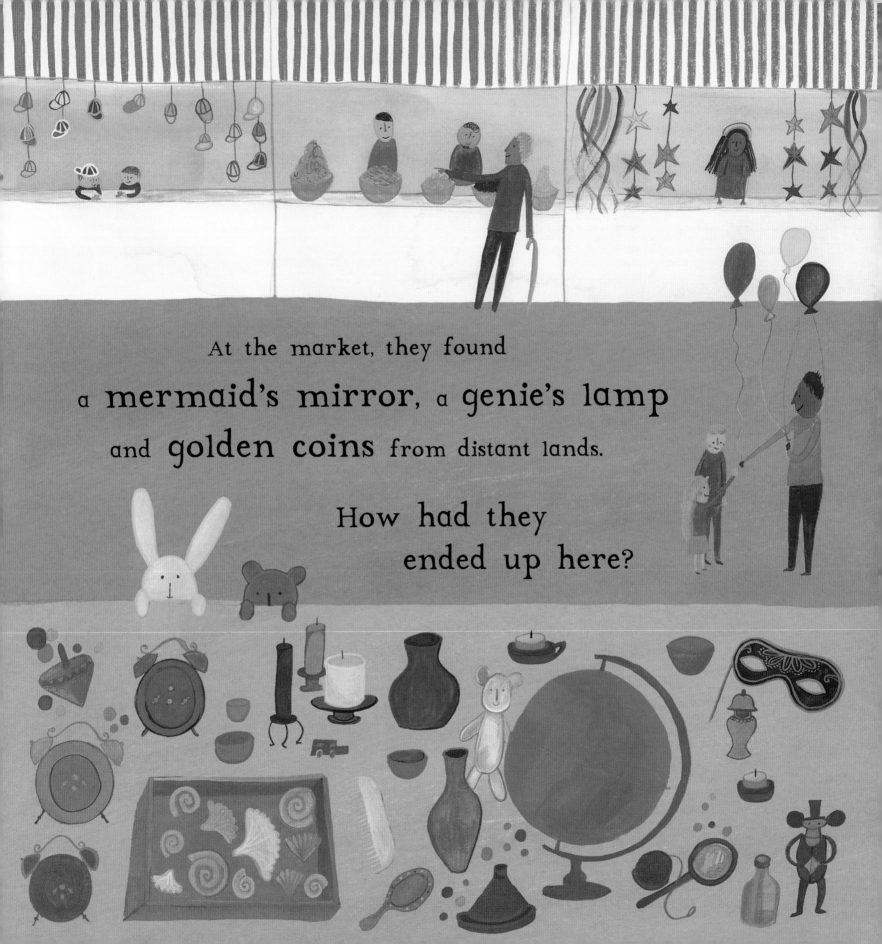

At the market, they found

a **mermaid's mirror**, a **genie's lamp** and **golden coins** from distant lands.

How had they ended up here?

When they got home,
Tilly was tired.
"I've got an idea!" said Mom.

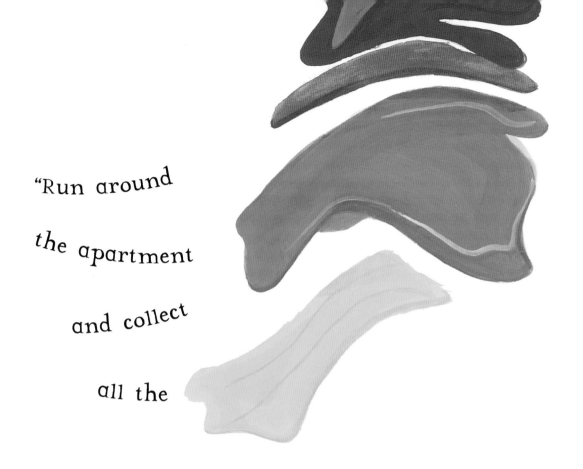

"Run around

the apartment

and collect

all the

sheets,

towels

and

blankets

you can find."

"Ta da!" Mom had made the most beautiful tent that Tilly had ever seen.

"Welcome to **our vacation home!**" laughed Mom.

Inside the **tent,**

they told **stories** all night.

Tilly was so happy.
It had been a **wonderful** adventure.

"I can't wait to tell my friends about **my staycation!**"

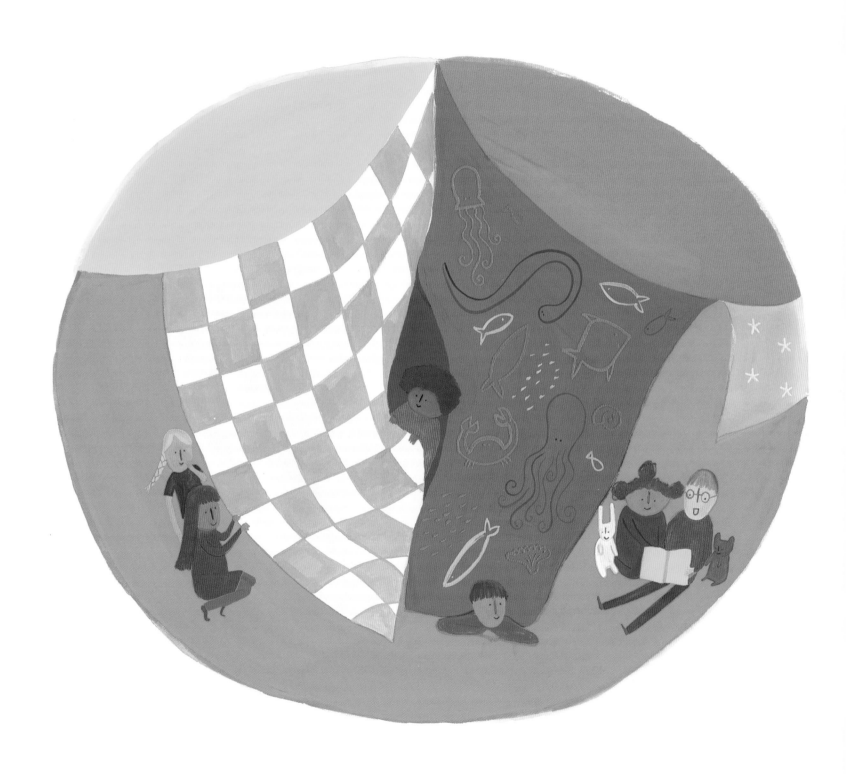

And she did!